Teggs is no ordinary dinosaur –
he's an **ASTROSAUR!** Captain of
the amazing spaceship DSS *Sauropod*,
he goes on dangerous missions and
fights evil – along with his faithful
crew, Gipsy, Arx and Iggy!

Collect all the **ASTROSAURS!**
Free collector cards in every book
for you to swap with your friends.
More cards available from the
ASTROSAURS website –
www.astrosaurs.co.uk

Read all the adventures of
Teggs, Gipsy, Arx and Iggy!

BOOK ONE:
RIDDLE OF THE RAPTORS

BOOK TWO:
THE HATCHING HORROR

BOOK THREE:
THE SEAS OF DOOM

BOOK FOUR:
THE MIND-SWAP MENACE

BOOK FIVE:
THE SKIES OF FEAR

BOOK SIX:
THE SPACE GHOSTS

BOOK SEVEN:
DAY OF THE DINO-DROIDS

Coming soon

BOOK NINE:
THE PLANET OF PERIL

Find out more at www.astrosaurs.co.uk

Astrosaurs

THE TERROR-BIRD TRAP

Steve Cole

Illustrated by Woody Fox

RED FOX

THE TERROR-BIRD TRAP
A RED FOX BOOK 978 0 099 48798 2 (from January 2007)
0 099 48798 5

First published in Great Britain by Red Fox,
an imprint of Random House Children's Books

This edition published 2006

1 3 5 7 9 10 8 6 4 2

Text copyright © Steve Cole, 2006
Cover illustration © Steve Richards/Dynamo Design, 2006
Inside illustrations copyright © Woody Fox, 2006
Map copyright © Charlie Fowkes

The right of Steve Cole to be identified as the author of this work
has been asserted in accordance with the Copyright, Designs and
Patents Act 1988.

Papers used by Random House Children's Books are natural,
recyclable products made from wood grown in sustainable forests.
The manufacturing processes conform to the environmental
regulations of the country of origin.

Typeset in Bembo Schoolbook by Palimpsest Book Production Limited,
Polmont, Stirlingshire

Red Fox Books are published by Random House Children's Books,
61–63 Uxbridge Road, London W5 5SA,
a division of The Random House Group Ltd,
in Australia by Random House Australia (Pty) Ltd,
20 Alfred Street, Milsons Point, Sydney, NSW 2061, Australia,
in New Zealand by Random House New Zealand Ltd,
18 Poland Road, Glenfield, Auckland 10, New Zealand,
and in South Africa by Random House (Pty) Ltd,
Isle of Houghton, Corner of Boundary Road & Carse O'Gowrie,
Houghton 2198, South Africa

THE RANDOM HOUSE GROUP Limited Reg. No. 954009
www.kidsatrandomhouse.co.uk

A CIP catalogue record for this book is available from the British Library.

Printed and bound in Great Britain by
Bookmarque Limited, Croydon, Surrey

For Kelly Cauldwell
Teggs's godmother and bringer of terror birds

WARNING!

THINK YOU KNOW ABOUT DINOSAURS?

THINK AGAIN!

The dinosaurs . . .

Big, stupid, lumbering reptiles. Right?

All they did was eat, sleep and roar a bit. Right?

Died out millions of years ago when a big meteor struck the Earth. Right?

Wrong!

The dinosaurs weren't stupid. They may have had small brains, but they used them well. They had big thoughts and big dreams.

By the time the meteor hit, the last dinosaurs had already left Earth for ever. Some breeds had discovered how to travel through space as early as the Triassic period, and were already enjoying a new life among the stars. No one has found evidence of dinosaur technology yet. But the first fossil bones were only unearthed in 1822, and new finds are being made all the time.

The proof is out there, buried in the ground.

And the dinosaurs live on, way out in space, even now. They've settled down in a place they call the Jurassic Quadrant and over the last sixty-five million years they've gone on evolving.

The dinosaurs we'll be meeting are

part of a special group called the Dinosaur Space Service. Their job is to explore space, to go on exciting missions and to fight evil and protect the innocent!

These heroic herbivores are not just dinosaurs.

They are *astrosaurs*!

NOTE: The following story has been translated from secret Dinosaur Space Service records. Earthling dinosaur names are used throughout, although some changes have been made for easy reading. There's even a guide to help you pronounce the dinosaur names at the back of the book.

THE CREW OF THE DSS SAUROPOD

**CAPTAIN
TEGGS STEGOSAUR**

ARX ORANO,
FIRST OFFICER

GIPSY SAURINE,
COMMUNICATIONS
OFFICER

IGGY TOOTH,
CHIEF ENGINEER

Jurassic Quadrant

Ankylos

Steggos

Diplox

INDEPENDE
DINOSAU
ALLIANC

vegetarian
sector

Squawk
Major

DSS
UNION OF
PLANETS

PTEROSAURI

Tri System

Corytho

Lambeos

Iguanos

Aqua Minor

Geldos Cluster

Teerex
Major

Olympus

TYRANNOSAUR
TERRITORIES

Planet Sixty

carnivore

Raptos

sector

THEROPOD EMPIRE

Megalos

Cryptos

vegmeat
zone

(neutral space)

SEA REPTILE
SPACE

Pliosaur
Nurseries

Not to scale

THE
TERROR-BIRD
TRAP

Chapter One

THE SHORE OF SECRETS

Captain Teggs Stegosaur stared out of the shuttle window at the picture-perfect view. Three suns lit the bright blue sky. The sea sparkled like it was full of emeralds. Tiny tropical islands lay dotted all around.

"So this is the planet Atlantos," he said, frowning. "It looks far too *nice* for a rough, tough mission. It's the sort of place you go to have a . . . a . . . "
He pulled a face, as if the words tasted bad. "A *holiday*!"

Gipsy Saurine, his stripy communications officer, playfully threw a beach ball at his head. "A little holiday wouldn't hurt you, Captain."

"Gipsy's right," said Iggy Tooth, his claws gripping the shuttle's joystick as he steered. "You haven't had a day off since you took charge of the *Sauropod*!"

The DSS *Sauropod* was the best ship in the Dinosaur Space Service, and Iggy the iguanodon was its chief engineer. Right now it was up in orbit, waiting for Teggs and his team of astrosaurs to return. They flew the *Sauropod* all around the galaxy – the dashing stegosaurus's appetite for adventure was even greater than his appetite for fresh ferns – and he ate those by the ton!

"Who needs a day off?" said Teggs. "Righting wrongs and fighting villains isn't hard work – it's fun!" He batted the beach ball over to Arx Orano, his triceratops deputy. "What do you think, Arx?"

Arx balanced the ball on the biggest of his three grey horns. "It's just a feeling, Captain, but I think this mission may be one of our most dangerous yet."

Teggs looked at Arx thoughtfully. The triceratops's instincts were strong, and if he smelled trouble ahead, he was probably right.

Hooray!

Iggy pointed to an island that was bigger than all the others. "There's our destination," he said. "Kleen Island."

"Well, we've got here at top speed in the shuttle, just as we were told," said Teggs. "Now all we need to know is *why*. I wish Admiral Rosso would hurry up and tell us." Rosso was the big-cheese barosaurus in charge of the entire DSS, who sent the astrosaurs on their missions.

"I'm sure he'll be in touch soon," said Gipsy. She picked up a bucket and spade. "And while we're waiting – we can *play!*"

Iggy landed the shuttle on a beautiful beach, and the astrosaurs went outside into the triple-sunshine. The place was deserted. While Arx and Iggy explored over by some steep white cliffs, Gipsy went paddling at the sea's edge. Teggs chased after her, splashing water over her with his big spiky tail. As he did so, he heard something crack beneath his feet.

"Hey, this isn't sand I'm standing on!" said Teggs, peering into the water. "It looks like . . . a tiled roof!"

Gipsy frowned. "Why would anyone lay a roof under water?"

"I don't know," said Teggs. He paddled over to the edge of the roof. Then he dipped his head beneath the waves for a few seconds and looked around. "A whole *street* has been built under here!" he spluttered, licking the salt from his lips. "Think of the problems the owners must have with damp!"

"Maybe that's why there's no one about," said Gipsy, glancing round nervously.

"Hey, Captain!" called Iggy, breaking the silence.

Teggs raced over. "What's up?"

Iggy showed him a large, sharp tooth. "Looks like something has been here before us."

Arx stared at Iggy's find. "This came from a carnivore," he said. "A very *large* carnivore."

"I wouldn't want to meet its owner." Gipsy shuddered. "Not unless *all* its teeth have fallen out!"

"If there are carnivores about, maybe that explains why no one is here," said Teggs. "We'd better get back to the shuttle and change into combat gear."

"So much for the holiday!" Iggy sighed as he started to lead the way back to their little ship.

Suddenly, the ground began to tremble beneath them. Then it lurched. The astrosaurs staggered sideways.

"What was *that*?" asked Iggy, as the tremors died away. "An earthquake?"

"I don't think so." Teggs frowned, shifting his weight between his four enormous feet. "The whole island feels like it's tipped to one side!"

Then a loud beep came from Gipsy's wrist communicator, followed by a lot of tweets and whistles. "It's the dimorphodon," she said. The dimorphodon were the *Sauropod*'s flight crew, little flying reptiles who worked the ship's controls. "They say that Admiral Rosso is ready to talk to us now."

10

"Tell them to beam his image over to the shuttle's scanner," said Teggs, striding back inside the little spaceship.

Gipsy whistled back to the dimorphodon in their own language and, a few moments later, Admiral Rosso's bespectacled face appeared on the scanner screen. Teggs saluted and the others crowded in around him.

"Sorry I couldn't speak to you about this mission sooner," said Rosso. "I wanted to be sure of the facts."

"What *are* the facts, sir?" Teggs asked.

"Kleen Island is the only island on Atlantos large enough to support life," Rosso began. "It's home to these peaceful creatures – bactrosaurs."

 A picture of a prim, duck-billed dinosaur appeared on the screen.

"I've heard of them," said Gipsy. "They are famous for being the cleanest dinosaurs in space."

"That's why they came to Atlantos," said Rosso. "They live a very clean and simple life. There's no pollution here. In fact, there's no technology of any kind."

"Imagine that!" gasped Iggy. "No technology! That means no spaceships, no engines, no computers, nothing noisy and oily and speedy . . ." He stuck out his tongue. "How boring!"

Rosso raised an eyebrow. "It might be boring to you, Iggy, but that's how the bactrosaurs like it. And so do the meat-eating megalodon – or the megs, for short!"

Teggs felt his spines tingle as the image of a massive shark-like creature now appeared on the scanner.

"A sea monster!" gasped Gipsy.

"That explains where the giant tooth came from," said Iggy. "It must have washed up from the ocean. But how come carnivores are sharing a world with plant-eaters?"

"Atlantos is in the Vegmeat Zone," Arx reminded him, "the no-man's land between the Vegetarian Sector and the Carnivore Sector. They have every right to be here."

"In fact, the megs were on Atlantos long before the bactrosaurs," said Rosso. "But since they can only live in the sea and not on dry land, they couldn't stop the bactrosaurs from taking Kleen Island. The two races

13

have reluctantly lived side by side for hundreds of years."

"So what's changed?" asked Teggs. "Why did we rush to get here?"

Rosso's face swam back into view on the screen. "The bactrosaurs' ruler, Queen Soapi, sent an urgent message to the DSS."

"I thought they had no technology," said Gipsy.

"They don't – she stuffed it in a bottle and used a giant catapult to send it into space." Rosso tutted. "It took six months to reach us!"

"Well?" Teggs was bursting with suspense. "What did she say?"

"She said that the whole island was sinking into the sea!" Rosso looked more serious than Teggs had ever seen him. "That's why I sent you along at once – while I checked her findings with space radar. The final results have just come in . . ."

Iggy gulped. "Was she right?"

Rosso nodded. "Almost half the island is now underwater!"

"So, that was no earthquake we felt just now," Arx realized. "That was the island sinking a little deeper."

"And that explains the roof we found beneath the water," said Gipsy. "It's just the top of a sunken building!"

"But whoever heard of a sinking island?" cried Teggs.

"Someone might be making it sink on purpose," said Rosso. "Your mission is to find out who and to stop them – before the bactrosaurs' home vanishes beneath the waves for good!"

Chapter Two

TERROR WITH A TWIST!

As Rosso's image faded from the scanner screen, Teggs led his crew back outside.

Arx had picked up a special detector. "With this I can measure the next shockwave, and see how quickly the island is sinking." He ducked into a nearby cave, and they could hear his feet splashing through water. "I'll set it up in here, out of the way."

"I bet the megs are behind this," said Iggy crossly. "They're probably fed up with sharing the planet with 'puny plant-eaters'. With Kleen Island underwater, the bactrosaurs will have nowhere else to go."

Gipsy nodded. "They'll have to leave Atlantos. The megs will get the whole planet to themselves!"

"But if it *is* them – *how* are they sinking the island?" said Arx, coming back out from the cave. "The megs are quite stupid even by carnivore standards. Plus, there's no technology here – they can't have built a rock-melting ray or a sea-bed smasher . . ."

17

"We must be sure of all the facts before we take any action," Teggs declared. "This is a serious situation. We can't afford to make any blunders."

"You already have!" came a loud, throaty squawk. "And it's the last one you shall ever make!"

Suddenly a huge, menacing creature burst out from behind a rock to block the astrosaurs' way. It stood upright on two strong legs. Its feet ended in terrifying talons. In place of arms it had thick, feathered wings. Its face was like that of a massive eagle, with glowing green eyes and a big, brutal beak.

"A terror bird!" gasped Arx. "Admiral Rosso didn't say anything about *them* being here!"

Three more of the massive, feathery monsters sprang out from caves in the cliff face. Teggs flexed his spiky tail, ready for a fight. Terror birds were named with good reason. They were

the biggest thugs in space, spreading fear, meanness and misery all across the Jurassic Quadrant.

"What are *you* doing here?" growled Teggs.

"The name's Gastro," the first terror bird announced. "And we don't speak to megalodon spies. I bet King Fin sent you here to sink the island even faster!"

"We aren't spies. We're astrosaurs!" Teggs protested.

"As if!" Gastro took a menacing step towards them, and glanced back at his gang. "Looks like we're going to have to teach these dinos a lesson, boys." Teggs reared up, ready for battle.

But, to his surprise, Gastro pulled a chalkboard from behind the rock and wrote: SINKING ISLANDS IS VERY NAUGHTY. The biggest bird produced a strange sort of guitar. It was made from string, spanners and an old sink plunger. He played it – very badly – while his friend squawked:

"Working for meg-aaa-lo-don
Is very naughty and not very nice!
Stop us sinking or else we will have to
Ask you not to in a very, very loud voice!"

Teggs scratched his head. "Well, I've never heard of terror birds singing to their enemies before!"

"I think I'd sooner fight them!" Iggy had covered his ears. "These jokers couldn't carry a tune in a bucket!"

"Had enough, eh?" Gastro smiled grimly. "Well, go back to your meg masters and tell them to stop sinking this island – or Gordon here will sing you the next fifty verses!"

"But you've got it all wrong!" cried Teggs.

"How dare you – Gordon wrote that song himself!" Gastro puffed out his feathery chest. "I can see I'm going to have to take very serious measures." Suddenly he pulled out a pointed dunce's cap. "Put this on your head and go and stand in that cave for five minutes."

"You're crazy!" cried Teggs, ducking as the terror bird tried to put the cap on his head.

"Wear it!" squawked Gastro.

"No!" Teggs grappled with the terror bird. He could feel the fearsome strength in Gastro's muscles — and yet the bird seemed careful not to hurt him. Iggy grabbed hold of Gastro too, and so Gordon grabbed hold of him. Gipsy responded by grabbing Gordon, and another terror bird grabbed her.

Teggs wasn't sure if they were having a fight or doing the conga!

But the next moment the slapdash struggle was halted by a humongous hoot: "*Stop!*"

At once, the terror birds fell to their knees, meek and mild.

Teggs turned to find that two figures had appeared on the beach behind them. He recognized them from Admiral Rosso's briefing — they were

bactrosaurs. One was plainly dressed in a white robe, but the other was wearing a crisp golden cape. A crown of shiny leaves sat on her head-crest, and she wore pink rubber gloves on her hooves.

"Hello!" said Teggs. "My name is Captain Teggs Stegosaur of the DSS *Sauropod*, and this is my crew." Gipsy, Arx and Iggy gathered round him. "You must be Queen Soapi."

"I am indeed," she said in a rather royal voice. "I thought I heard a horrible, dirty, old spaceship arrive so I came to investigate."

"Dirty? What a cheek!" Iggy grumbled.

Gipsy nudged him in the ribs. "You mean, 'What a cheek, *Your Majesty*!'"

"I hope you're not fighting on my island," Queen Soapi went on. "It's rough, and dirty. I mean, just look at your uniform, Teggs. It's all mucky!" She turned to the other bactrosaur. "Janice, my hoof-maiden, wash down the captain!"

Janice swiftly attacked Teggs's top with a bucket of warm soapy water and a scrubbing brush.

"Hey! That tickles!" Teggs protested.

"Now, who else needs a quick scrub?" said Queen Soapi. "Perhaps I should spray you *all* with disinfectant, just to be on the safe side."

"Please, Your Majesty, we weren't fighting," said Gastro. "The lads and I were just trying to stop these sharky spies being so naughty. They expect us to believe they are astrosaurs!"

"You silly big birds," said Queen Soapi fondly. "I'm sure you meant well, Gastro, but these *are* astrosaurs — come to help us in our hour of need! I sent for them ages ago."

"You did?" Gastro narrowed his eyes at Teggs. "Oh. It seems I owe you all an apology." He bowed down to the astrosaurs. "I am truly sorry. I was only trying to protect our little island."

"*Our* little island?" Gipsy couldn't believe what she was hearing.

"These terror birds live here," Queen Soapi explained. "They have done so for almost a year."

"But they're carnivores!" cried Iggy.

"Other terror birds are," said Gastro, "but *we* are vegetarian." As if to prove the point he uprooted a clump of sea-grass and gobbled it down. "Mmm," he said, licking his sandy beak.

"You see?" said Queen Soapi. "And in return for a place to stay, he and his five friends have installed flush toilets all over Atlantos."

"We were just checking the pipes in this area when we saw you on the beach," Gastro explained. "I'm afraid we jumped to conclusions."

"No real harm done," Teggs said politely. "But what's this about flush toilets? I thought any sort of technology was banned on Atlantos?"

"One tiny exception," Queen Soapi admitted. "Gastro's toilets have made our lives shinier, more sparkly and cleaner than ever! Such lovely toilets are the only things that keep us cheerful as we go on sinking."

"On the *Sauropod*, every toilet trip helps to power our ship," said Iggy brightly. "We all poo in a big hole above the engine room!"

Janice the hoof-maiden fainted instantly and fell headfirst into her soapy bucket. Queen Soapi went an alarming shade of green. "Don't be so filthy!" she cried. "Janice, wake up at once and wash that iguanodon's mouth out!"

When Iggy opened his mouth to protest, Janice stuck her scrubbing brush in it.

Gastro beamed. "Well, we'd better finish those checks, boys," he told his friends. "Report back to me when you've finished."

"Yes, Gastro," squawked the three terror birds, and they lumbered back to the caves they had come from.

Teggs was still watching Gastro closely. "With the island sinking, why do you stay?"

"Our own ship has broken down. We *can't* leave. And anyway – we haven't got anywhere else to go!" Gastro sighed. "We had to leave our own planet because we weren't like the other terror birds. While they all went hunting for meat, we cooked veggie-burgers. While they were off being scary and mean around the galaxy, we trained to be plumbers so we could help people." He wiped a tear from his glittering green eye.

"Our rulers tried to lock us up for giving terror birds a bad name. We have been wanted birds ever since."

"But I admire anyone who dares to be different," said Queen Soapi. "I am glad to have them as my honoured guests."

She tickled Gastro under the beak. Then, suddenly, the whole island started to shake. With a lurch, it tipped to one side just as before.

The sea surged further up the shore towards them like a huge, hungry animal.

"We're sinking again!" wailed Queen Soapi, wiping her eyes with a carefully ironed tissue. "My people – and my dear little terror birds – are doomed!"

"Not now the astrosaurs are here," said Teggs firmly. "Whatever's going on, we're going to stop it!"

"And we can start by checking my detector," said Arx. "That shockwave will have given me loads of vital info!" He galloped into the nearby cave where he'd left his gadget.

But just seconds later, he gave a bloodcurdling yell . . .

Chapter Three

THE WHOLE TOOTH

"Arx is in trouble!" cried Teggs, already bounding towards the dark entrance. "Follow me!" He splashed into the flooded cave, Gipsy and Iggy right behind him. "Arx, are you all right?"

The triceratops staggered towards them. "Something bit me! I didn't see what."

Iggy crouched beside him. "Hey! There's a splinter in your leg."

"That's no splinter," said Gipsy, boggling in amazement. "It's a tooth, like the one we found on the beach!"

Teggs plucked it out gently. "It's a megalodon tooth!"

"Bless my horns," cried Arx, shaking his sore leg. "It certainly looks like it!"

"These caves are full of potholes," Gastro explained. "Now the ground is underwater, the megs can swim up and attack."

"Why, those sneaky, super-sized sharks!" cried Iggy crossly.

"If I ever catch one of them, I'll . . . I'll" – Gastro struggled to find a fitting punishment – "I'll read it a lovely hundred-page poem Gordon wrote about how all prehistoric beasts should live in harmony."

Teggs pulled a face. "Boring a meg to death won't stop the island from sinking."

Then everyone jumped as an ear-splitting cry echoed around the cave. A terror bird came rushing from out of the darkness — or rather, a *terrified* bird.

"Godfrey!" gasped Gastro. "I didn't know you were in here."

"Neither did I," said Arx.

"I – I – I was checking the pipes round the corner," Godfrey stammered. "Then this huge big shark-thing popped out of a pothole and tried to chomp me! Look!" He unfurled his wing to reveal yet another jagged tooth.

"Those megs should see a deep-sea dentist," said Gipsy. "Their teeth are falling out all over the place!"

"We know a lovely song about cleaning your teeth," said Gastro brightly.

"Let's get back to the beach," said Teggs quickly, before the terror birds could launch into another musical number. "We don't want the megs trying to floss with anyone else's ankle!"

The astrosaurs and the terror birds came quickly out of the cave and back to the beach. Janice promptly fainted again, and Queen Soapi hooted with horror. "Look how messy you are!"

"The megs are growing bolder," Gastro warned her. "They are attacking anyone who goes into those caves."

"But *why*?" cried the queen.

"Have you tried asking them?" said Teggs.

"Certainly not!" she snapped. "I have vowed never to speak to King Fin and his sharky subjects ever again."

"How come?" asked Gipsy.

"Because he broke the truce between the land and the sea, that's why!" Queen Soapi trembled at the memory.

"Many years ago, two of my hoof-maidens went swimming in the sea. They swam out too far so they called for help. Suddenly, two megs came zooming up to them, jaws wide open – trying to eat them, if you please! We had to fight them off. We barely got those poor hoof-maidens back alive!"

"How horrible," said Arx with sympathy.

"It gets worse," said the queen. "Not long after, we found two of those smelly, sharky monsters wriggling up the shore of this very beach."

Teggs frowned. "Were they trying to invade you?"

"We didn't stop to ask," she said. "We simply pushed them back into the sea with long poles so we didn't have to touch the slimy things. And that was the last we heard of them for twenty years!"

"Until now," said Iggy.

"What a nasty lot." Gastro shook his head sadly. "Well, I suppose we must clear the caves in case they attack again. Come on, Godfrey, let's tell the others to stop checking the pipes."

Teggs watched the two terror birds go. "You know, I've just had a thought."

Queen Soapi looked worried. "It's not a dirty thought, is it?"

"No! I just realized – the island only started sinking once the terror birds arrived here. And, so far, the megs have only attacked the caves where the terror birds go."

Gipsy gasped. "You mean, if the megs *are* sinking the island, they might not be after the bactrosaurs at all?"

"Right," said Teggs. "They could be trying to get Gastro and the terror birds for giving carnivores a bad name!"

Janice squeaked, and then fainted again. "Get up, dear," said Queen Soapi wearily. "You'll get dirty down there!"

"It's an interesting theory, Captain," said Arx. "But how would the megs have heard of Gastro and his friends in the first place?"

"Good point, Arx," Teggs agreed. "They might be innocent sharks. In which case, some other evil force is at work on Atlantos."

Janice, who had just woken up, quickly fainted again.

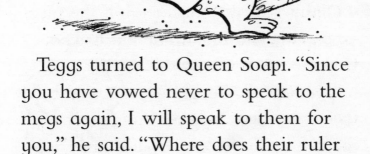

Teggs turned to Queen Soapi. "Since you have vowed never to speak to the megs again, I will speak to them for you," he said. "Where does their ruler live?"

"King Fin's under-sea palace is about a mile from here," said Queen Soapi.

"I'd like to come with you, Captain," said Gipsy instantly.

Teggs smiled. "Iggy, while we are away, think about ways to defend this island. We don't know when the megs will attack again!"

Iggy saluted. "First I'll fetch the two auto-swimsuits from the shuttle. You will need those to swim underwater."

"Thanks," said Teggs. "As for you, Arx — we need to know *how* the island is being sunk. Maybe then we can do something to stop it."

"And there's not a moment to lose, Captain." Arx was studying his detector again. "Now that more than half the island is underwater, the sea bed is very weak. We will sink faster and faster."

Gipsy gulped. "How long have we got?"

"I'll need to run more tests to know for sure," said Arx. "Maybe a few weeks, maybe a few days . . . or maybe just a few hours!"

Queen Soapi was speechless with shock. Janice, though she was still in a faint, stuck her legs up in the air.

"We'd better get going," said Teggs. "Fast!"

Chapter Four

BATTLE BENEATH THE SEA

Iggy rushed to fetch the auto-swimsuits. They were his own invention. The big, orange puffy suits stopped the heavy astrosaurs sinking, while powerful built-in motors propelled them through the water.

Soon, Teggs and Gipsy were trying them on at the ocean's edge.

"We could have used these special suits when we were stuck on the sea bed on Aqua Minor," said Gipsy, shivering at the memory.

"I look like a big orange blob!" Teggs declared. He bobbed up and down in the water, trying to get used to it.

Iggy smiled. "This reminds me of a rude rhyme I once heard!" He cleared his throat and began:

"There once was a bold stegosaurus
Who frolicked upon the seashore-us
Though he didn't oughtta
He weed in the water
And left the fish in an uproar-us!"

Teggs couldn't help but chuckle. Good old Iggy was always trying to cheer people up, even when things were very serious – or in this case, *sea*-rious. As he gazed out across the ocean, Teggs couldn't help feeling that they were being watched – that something out there in the depths knew they were coming.

Arx, Queen Soapi, Janice and Gastro all came to the beach to wave them off.

"How do you know the megs won't simply eat you?" twittered the queen.

"Because we are astrosaurs, and we come in peace," said Gipsy. "We only want to hear their side of the story."

Teggs and Gipsy waved goodbye, then pressed a button on their suits.

With a spark, a splash and a "Wheeeeee!" they started swishing away through the sea.

They soon got used to the auto-swimsuits. It was like someone else was doing all the hard work for you, so swimming underwater became good fun.

From here they could see just how much of the island had already slipped beneath the waves. They swam along submerged streets and over sunken sandy gardens. It was like an eerie under-sea town, empty of all life.

Then the water got dirtier. Big brown lumps floated in it like a nasty soup.

Gipsy turned up her snout inside her helmet. "Is that dung?"

"I think so," said Teggs. "Looks like the megs aren't as fussy as the bactrosaurs when it comes to keeping clean!"

They swam on and on through the murky, mucky water.

Then, suddenly, Teggs saw a huge dark shape cut through the sea towards him. It was grey and sleek like a shark but much, much larger. The fin on its back was as big as a sail. Its jaws were open wide and bristling with teeth.

Teggs gulped and switched off his propellers. "I think we've met our first megalodon!"

Another of the fearsome creatures approached and loomed over Gipsy.

"Greetings," said Gipsy. "We are astrosaurs. We come in peace!"

"You come in *filth*!" cried the meg. "You want to protect those fools on Kleen Island. You're on their side."

Teggs swam up to him. "So, you admit that you are sinking the island?"

"We're not talking to him," the other meg told Gipsy. "He laughs at rude poems about making the sea dirty. Like it's not already dirty enough!"

"But that poem was just a silly joke!" she said. "Captain Teggs would never really wee in the sea!"

"Of course not! I used a flush toilet before we set off!" Teggs informed him. "Why are you attacking the island? Are you trying to get the terror birds?"

But the megs were too angry to listen to another word.

"You make *everything* mucky, you dino-dirtbags!" said the first one. "But pretty soon your friends will be well and truly sunk – all of them."

"We're gonna get them good," added the second. "Especially that gutless Gastro – just you wait!"

Then Teggs felt sharp teeth on his tail. One of the megs must have sneaked up behind him!

His auto-swimsuit made a very rude noise – it was punctured. Teggs started to deflate like a giant orange balloon. The air rushed from his suit and sent him whizzing off in a wild, helpless zigzag through the sewage-filled sea.

"No!" Teggs cried. "Gipsyyyyyyyyy!"

He knew he was leaving her to face the megs alone. He paddled desperately to try to reach her, but the air-leak was forcing him further and further away.

Then he hit something with an almighty CRASH! To his astonishment it was a brick wall! He had gone smashing into one of the sunken buildings on the island's coast. And as the last pockets of air spluttered from his suit, he could feel himself sinking too.

Teggs started to swim as hard as he could. He whirled his tail around and around like a spiky propeller with all his strength, forcing himself upwards, *upwards*.

Finally he broke the surface of the water and a big wave washed him onto the shore. Queen Soapi, Janice, Gastro and Iggy were still there waiting for him.

"What happened?" said Iggy, helping him up.

Queen Soapi cringed. "Perhaps you should have a bath before you tell me, you look terribly dirty—"

"This is no time to worry about washing!" Teggs shouted. "The megs have got Gipsy, and they want to get us all – especially you, Gastro! Unless we can find help fast, it looks like we are *all* well and truly sunk!"

Chapter Five

A SOGGY SURPRISE

"Those monstrous, mucky megs!" cried Queen Soapi, as Janice fainted again. "I must tell my people this terrible news at once."

Teggs nodded and pulled out his communicator. "And I must tell Arx."

"I've run lots of tests," said the triceratops. "No luck yet, Captain."

"Well, *I've* had some luck," Teggs retorted. "And it's all bad! Get down to the beach, fast!"

When Arx heard the news about Gipsy, his horns drooped. "We must contact DSS HQ, Captain," he said. "We will need reinforcements to get

Gipsy back, and rescue ships to take
everyone safely off this island."

But Queen Soapi
shook her head.
"No! This is our
home, and we will
fight to protect it."

"Perhaps the
boys and I should
move somewhere else," said Gastro.
"With us out of the way, maybe the
megs will leave you alone."

"You cannot go," Queen Soapi
insisted. "You are VIPs – Very
Important Plumbers – and we shall
defend you to the end. I will tell my
people to finish making their Spotless
Survival Suits and coconut catapults at
top speed."

Teggs frowned. "Spotless Survival
Suits?"

"I came up with the idea as soon as
we heard the island was sinking," said

Gastro proudly. "The suits use technology taken from our ship. They are waterproof and inflatable so, if we all go under, even the heaviest dinosaur can stay afloat. They are also tooth-proof, claw-proof, stain-proof—"

"I'd like to *see* proof!" said Iggy grumpily. "They sound too good to be true!"

"I'll show you if you like," said Gastro. "Soon every single bactrosaur will be safe and snug inside one."

Queen Soapi patted his head. "Best of all, they are made of a special material that dirt can't stick to, so they stay spotless!" Janice woke up and nodded eagerly. "And a good job too. Those nasty, slimy, super-sharks are so *dirty*! I mean, have you *seen* the state of their water?"

"Yes," said Teggs. "Although they don't seem very happy about it either."

Just then, the island lurched and shook as it sank even *deeper* into the sea. Seconds earlier, the water had come up to Teggs's ankles. Now it was up to his hips! He splashed out onto the beach in alarm. Janice yelped and hooted – then quickly fainted for about the fourteenth time.

"We're going down faster and faster!" cried Queen Soapi.

"I'll call Admiral Rosso from the shuttle's long-range space radio, right away," said Teggs. "Arx, come with me. Iggy, do you think you can fix my auto-swimsuit?"

"Not without a special needle and thread," said Iggy glumly.

Gastro patted him with a friendly wing. "I'm sure we will have what you need at the Spotless Survival Suit workshop."

The queen smiled. "You can check out our suits and fix your own at the same time!"

"Sounds great," said Teggs. "We'll join you there later."

"Meanwhile, I must go to the palace and speak to my people in their hour of need," said Queen Soapi. "Gastro, would you be a dear and carry Janice back to her room for me?"

"Of course, Your Majesty," said Gastro. His mighty muscles rippled with strength as he lifted the helpless hoof-maiden. Teggs was glad the terror bird was on his side!

Without another word, he and Arx hurried off towards the shuttle.

But a big surprise awaited them. The shuttle was bobbing about on the ocean waves like a rubber duck in a giant's bath!

"The island is sinking so quickly that our landing site is already underwater." Arx explained. "Luckily for us, the shuttle floats!"

But unluckily, the door was hanging open . . .

"Oh, no!" said Teggs, wading through the water towards the little spaceship. "I hope everything's still working!"

It wasn't. The astrosaurs soon saw that the shuttle had been wrecked! Water sloshed about on the floor. All the controls had been destroyed, and the space radio was smashed into a hundred pieces. Even Teggs's emergency supply of ferns had been scattered into the sea. He quickly guzzled up the few leaves still remaining.

"Who could have done such a thing?" Arx spluttered.

"I know!" said Teggs grimly. "Dipping ferns in salty water ruins the flavour!"

Arx frowned. "Um, I was talking about the damage done to the shuttle, Captain."

"Oh. Er, yes." Teggs quickly swallowed his food. "Well, I'll give you one guess." He pointed to a large white spike left behind in a ruined control panel.

It was a megalodon tooth!

"Nice try, shark brains," Teggs shouted out to sea. "But if we can't contact Admiral Rosso ourselves, the dimorphodon can do it for us. I'll call them on my communicator."

But all he heard back was the harsh, empty sound of space static.

"Uh-oh," said Arx. "Someone is blocking our signal with a powerful jamming device."

"But who?" said Teggs. "I thought the megs had no technology?"

The triceratops frowned. "It seems that we have underestimated them."

"Well, right now I estimate we're in big, big trouble." Teggs crossly whumped his tail against the soggy shuttle. "We've lost Gipsy, we can't get reinforcements, and now we've got no way of getting Gastro *or* the bactrosaurs off Kleen Island."

"I know," said Arx. "It seems the megs have caught us all together in their terror-bird trap!"

Chapter Six

TERROR DOWN THE TOILET

High on the cliff tops, in the gardens of Queen Soapi's palace, Iggy was walking with Gastro. The terror bird was carrying Janice the hoof-maiden to her room while the queen told her people the bad news about the megs.

Suddenly, Janice wriggled in his arms. "Are you all right?" asked Gastro. The hoof-maiden nodded quickly and got down.

Then she trotted giddily away, bumping into a bush as she went.

"Funny girl," Iggy said, and Gastro agreed. "Now then, how about taking me to the Spotless Survival Suit workshop?"

The workshop was a gleaming white building surrounded by perfect hedgerows. Through the window, Iggy could see all five of the other terror birds hard at work as they sang a tuneless little ditty about what fun it was to sew. Gordon and Godfrey's claws were a blur as they stitched the suits with their trim little talons.

"My boys are devoted to finishing the Survival Suits on time," Gastro explained. "They all love the bactrosaurs. If they're not checking the toilet pipes, they're in here working."

"Can I go inside and see the suits like Soapi said?" asked Iggy eagerly.

"First you must have a good wash," said Gastro. "No one's allowed inside unless they're spotless!" He pointed to some bathrooms nearby.

"Cheek!" Iggy fumed as he crossed the square. "I'm as clean as a carrot!"

The bathrooms were bright and well lit. Through a doorway, Iggy spotted a large, white china seat with a hole in it. "A flush toilet!" he declared. "I suppose I may as well give it a go."

He perched his scaly bottom on it, careful to keep his tail up in the air.

But then something *grabbed hold* of his bottom and pulled hard!

"Argh!" Iggy shouted in surprise. And before he could mutter another word he was dragged right down the toilet!

It was too dark to see what had grabbed hold of him. With a bump and a bounce and a *bang-bang-BANG* he went tumbling through a maze of slimy pipes. Finally, with a stinky SPLAT he fell out into a very nasty brown puddle.

"Well, now I really *do* need a shower," he groaned. "I wish I'd grabbed a Spotless Survival Suit first – this would be the perfect test!"

He looked around. He was in a dark, dirty tunnel. "Any megs hiding around here?" Iggy yelled, putting on his stun claws. "I'll turn you into shark paste!"

Then he heard a squelching, slithering, slurping noise coming from round the corner, as if a mile-wide slug was dragging itself towards him.

"Who – who's there?" said Iggy nervously, raising his fists.

But this was one enemy he couldn't fight – a huge landslide of stinky sludge! It filled the tunnel as it surged towards him, ready to engulf everything in its path.

Iggy turned and ran for his life . . .

★   ★   ★

Meanwhile, in a small under-sea cave, Gipsy's eyes fluttered open. She remembered the megs closing in around her, and Captain Teggs yelling her name. She had tried to swim away from the enormous super-sharks, but had crashed into some coral and knocked herself out.

Now she saw that there were bars blocking her way – she was a prisoner. Through the bars she could see a splendid cavern, covered in red and gold seaweed. Then a dark shape swam up in front of the entrance.

It was a huge meg with a bright gold crown perched upon his smooth head. Two slightly smaller fin-maidens bobbed about behind him in the blue water.

"I am King Fin," burbled the regal creature. "And you are my prisoner. Confess your crimes, landlubber!"

Gipsy frowned.
"But I haven't done anything. I only came here to talk to you."

"Rubbish!" sneered King Fin. "You are a landlubber spy for those ugly brutes up on dry land. First you try to drive us away, now you are planning a full-on attack!"

"What attack?" spluttered Gipsy. "You're the ones who attacked those bactrosaurs who swam too far out to sea."

"We were only trying to help them," said King Fin sniffily. "We tried to carry them back to shore, and the silly things went crazy!"

"Really?" Gipsy frowned. "You mean you weren't trying to eat them?"

"Ugh!" said King Fin. "We eat fish, not smelly, dirty dinosaurs!"

"Well, what about when you tried to wriggle up onto the beach?" said Gipsy.

The king glared at her. "Two of my fin-maidens were washed up there after a storm. They asked for help, and what did they get? A poke with a pole!"

"Oh dear," said Gipsy. "I think there's been a terrible misunderstanding here. Why didn't you explain to Queen Soapi what had happened?"

"After the way she treated my people?" He pushed his smooth grey nose up in the air. "I have vowed never to talk to her again!"

"But why are you attacking the island now?" Gipsy asked.

"We are going to get that gutless Gastro," King Fin hissed. "He is a traitor to his own people."

Gipsy gulped. "Then it *is* a terror-bird trap!"

"And as for his bactrosaur buddies . . . They started this dirty war, but they will soon find it's going to get a lot dirtier!"

"What do you mean?" said Gipsy. "Queen Soapi didn't start anything. *You* did."

"Don't be cheeky." King Fin waved at one of his fin-maidens, who swam quickly away. "You came here to spy on our top-secret weapon, didn't you?" he burbled. "Well, I'll show it to you myself. Tremble in fear at the sight of . . . the *tank-tank*!"

Suddenly, Gipsy heard the roar of an engine, and the sound of something heavy rumbling closer. She saw the fin-maiden was now floating inside a very curious contraption. It looked like a large aquarium on big, chunky wheels. Two huge guns stuck out from either side.

"Wonderful, isn't it?" King Fin swum and shimmied about it in excitement. "Part fish tank, part *real* tank. With these we can drive onto the island and get *all* you landlubbers!"

Gipsy felt her head-crest flush blue with alarm. "Drive *onto* it? I thought you were trying to *sink* it?"

"Shut up, stripy!" King Fin shook his tail. "Look! See these guns? They fire deadly dollops of dung! That'll teach those yukky bactrosaurs not to mess with us."

"But they don't *want* to mess with you!" Gipsy protested. "If you and Queen Soapi would only talk to each other—"

"The time for talking is over," said the king.

"Hang on, where did you *get* this tank-tank thing?" Gipsy demanded. "I didn't think you had any technology."

"You thought wrong then, didn't you?" King Fin retorted. "Fin-maidens, there are now enough tank-tanks for all of us. We shall all become *mega-megs*! Gather my army in the meeting-cave. I shall give my greatest ever speech . . . and then we shall strike!"

Gipsy's heart was sinking faster than Kleen Island. She knew that a dreadful battle was looming. And, while she was stuck in here, she was helpless to stop it!

Chapter Seven

IN THE DUNG!

Teggs was very worried as he stomped across the beach with Arx. "How can we stop King Fin's army of super-sharks with nothing but coconut catapults? And what about Gipsy?"

"I hope Iggy can fix your auto-swimsuit quickly," said Arx. "If only we had brought extra costumes! Then he and I could come with you."

"Wait!" Teggs stopped still. His keen eyes had noticed something grey peeping over the top of a large rock. "See that?"

"Could be a meg," Arx whispered. "One that has learned to live on dry land!"

"Maybe it can help us find Gipsy," said Teggs, and with a fierce growl he charged towards it. One strike of his powerful tail pulverized the rock – but there was no megalodon hiding behind it. Only a bundle of grey, shiny material.

Arx prodded it with his biggest horn. "It's a kind of auto-swimsuit!"

Teggs beamed. "Just what we need! Brilliant!"

"But where did it come from?" said Arx. "Let's smooth it out a bit . . ."

As they did so, it became clear that the suit was the same shape as an extra-big meg.

"I don't get it," said Teggs. "Since when did a shark need a swimsuit?"

"Look, Captain." Arx pointed behind him. "That rock was hiding a hole in the cliff face." He pulled lumps of rock away to reveal a dark cave-mouth. "It must be a secret tunnel. I wonder where it leads?"

"Let's find out," said Teggs, squeezing into the gap. "Phwoar! What a stink! It's worse than a sewer!"

The narrow passage seemed to go on for miles. The smell got worse the deeper they went.

"I think my nose is going to fall off!" Arx gasped.

The tunnel turned out to be a kind of side street, leading to a much larger, slimier tunnel. As soon as they entered it, a spooky noise came out of the darkness: "*Woahhhhhhhhhhh!*"

It was Iggy! He came charging out of the darkness like a thousand raptors were snapping at his tail. He ran straight into Teggs and Arx, and all three of them fell down in a bundle of legs, tails and horns.

"Iggy!" gasped Teggs, pulling the tip of the iguanodon's tail from his nostril. "Where did you spring from?"

"Quick, Captain," gasped Iggy. "We've got to get out of here!"

A huge, brown, stinky, sludgy, slimy tidal wave was gurgling towards them.

"Into the side tunnel!" cried Teggs.

He and Arx grabbed hold of Iggy and dived back into the hole they had come through – just before the thick, sewer-stinking sludge could swallow them up.

"It's bactrosaur poo!" Iggy explained.

"Mixed in with millions of gallons of bactrosaur wee! These tunnels are sewage pipes leading from the bactrosaurs' flush toilets. I was sucked down one of them – that's how I got here."

"Disgusting!" cried Arx. "Toilet mess should be recycled safely and cleanly, not dumped down here to make a dung mountain!"

Suddenly, the tunnel lurched and shook and tilted. "Uh-oh! The island is sinking again!" shouted Teggs.

"Aha!" cried Arx. "I understand now – it's the *dung*! Don't you see?"

"I see it all right," said Iggy. Already the sticky brown sludge was beginning to seep into the narrow passage.

"No, I mean *that* is why we are sinking!" Arx was hopping from foot to foot in excitement. "The toilets were built about a year ago, right? And ever since then, tons and tons of niffy nasties have been pouring down the pipes into these underground caves every day. *The sheer weight of all this untreated dung is making the island sink!*"

Teggs stared at Arx in amazement. "So the megs *aren't* sinking the island after all . . . It's Gastro and his dodgy plumbing!"

"And that explains why the megs are so angry," Arx added. "As the island sinks deeper, the dung is leaking out into the sea . . . polluting the waters for miles around!"

"No wonder they're ready to go to war," said Iggy. "So much for those terror birds being Very Important Plumbers! How could Gastro do such a rotten job?"

"Maybe someone has sabotaged the sewer system," Arx suggested. "Just like they sabotaged the shuttle."

"I wonder . . ." Teggs felt a shiver go down him from the tip of his tail to the top of his toes. "I just wonder . . ."

In the dark, murky depths of King Fin's domain, the invasion of Kleen Island was ready to begin.

Gipsy could hear the growl and rumble of hundreds of tank-tanks as they trundled away across the sea bed.

Soon the megs would reach the shores of Kleen Island. The bactrosaurs would stand no chance against the tank-tanks' deadly dung-shooters. How had a race of super-sharks built such dreadful weapons when they had no other technology? She knew she must find out – and warn Queen Soapi before it was too late.

So while the megs were busy, Gipsy picked the lock of her cage with a sharp shell and a stiff strip of seaweed.

"Yes!" she hooted, as the lock burst open.

But even as she sneaked away, a huge, fat megalodon swam into the palace chamber. It saw her at once.

Gipsy raised her hooves, ready for combat. "I don't want to fight," she insisted, "but we *must* stop your king. He's about to make a big mistake!"

"Bigger than you think," said the meg. "But not as big as the mistake you astrosaurs made in coming here . . ."

As the monster swam closer, Gipsy frowned to see a large zipper running down the length of its body. This wasn't a real meg, it was someone in a costume!

"I've come here to clear up any loose ends," chortled the fake-finned impostor. "And that includes *you*!"

Gipsy didn't recognize the voice, but she recognized the terrifying talons that sprang from the shark-suit.

She was all alone against a terror bird!

With an evil squawk, it reached out to get her . . .

Chapter Eight

LET BATTLE BEGIN!

"Guys, I reckon that Gastro has tricked us all!" Teggs looked gravely at Iggy and Arx. "He's been using dung to weigh down the island and stir up the megs. And at the same time he's been faking those cave attacks to stir up the bactrosaurs!"

"Then it wasn't a real meg that attacked me in the cave," realized Arx. "It was an impostor. Probably that goofy Godfrey wearing the shark swimsuit we found on the beach – he was hiding in the cave too, remember?"

84

"With a wingful of stolen shark teeth," Teggs growled. "I never trusted those overgrown canaries. I'll bet one of them smashed up our shuttle so we couldn't get help. Then another one swam after me and Gipsy to stop us learning the truth – that the terror birds are trying to start a war between the megs and the bactrosaurs!"

"But there's one thing I still don't understand," said Iggy. "Gastro and all five of his terror-bird chums were at the Survival-Suit workshop when I went to the bathroom," Iggy explained. "So how could one of them have pulled me down the toilet?"

"If there are more terror birds here than Gastro's been letting on, we'd better *flush* them out – and fast." Teggs gave a crooked smile. "Come on, boys, we must find Queen Soapi before it's too late. We've got a war to stop!"

But what Teggs didn't realize was that Queen Soapi was already ready for action.

She stood in the palace courtyard, watching as her warriors and hoof-maidens carefully washed their coconuts and catapults. Then they started to climb daintily into their Spotless Survival Suits, helped by some of the terror birds.

"We shall stand guard on the shore," Queen Soapi announced. "If the invaders so much as poke their sharky noses out of the ocean, we shall be ready for them!"

The bactrosaurs hooted and cheered – not at the thought of fighting shark-monsters, but because they were all rather taken with their dazzling new outfits.

Gastro bowed down before Queen Soapi. "It is time to put on your own Spotless Survival Suit, Your Majesty."

She nodded. "Thank you, Gastro. Whatever happens today, I am proud to have known you. You are a true friend to all bactrosaurs."

Gastro smiled. "Don't mention it," he said.

Gipsy dodged aside as the monster tried to grab her.

"I might have guessed," she said. "You terror birds have been helping the megs! Which one are you?"

"Gordon," said the disguised bird. "But, just to be fair, we've been helping the bactrosaurs too. See, the boss wants Queen Soapi and King Fin to battle each other."

"Why?" Gipsy demanded.

"There are too few of us to invade this planet," Gordon explained, lunging forwards. "So we will just stand back and let the bactrosaurs and the megs wipe each other out. See, the boss has made sure that this battle will end in a draw!" He chuckled. "Or do I mean a *dead* heat? Anyway, as the only people left on Atlantos, we will happily inherit it – without lifting a wing!"

Gipsy ducked beneath him. "The DSS will stop you."

"They can't. As far as the rest of the universe is concerned, this fight was nothing to do with us!" Gordon swiped at her with his talons, missing her by millimetres. "We simply stepped in to take the planet once it was empty."

"But what about the terror birds back home?" Gipsy reminded him. "Or was that story about being wanted a big lie?"

"No it was true all right." Gordon grimaced. "But the boss is going to take care of that," said Gordon. "Just like *I* am going to take care of *you*."

Gordon's claws slashed through the water once more as he bore down on Gipsy.

★   ★   ★

Teggs, Arx and Iggy burst out of the cave in the cliff face and rushed along the beach.

"We must warn Queen Soapi about what's really happening," puffed Teggs.

"Too late," said Arx, skidding to a halt as he rounded a sand dune. "Look!"

An army of bactrosaurs in gleaming white uniforms were trooping down the beach, led by four terror birds. They all carried catapults and coconuts. Queen Soapi marched at the back with Gastro and Janice the hoof-maiden.

"We must guard every cave!" Soapi cried. "If you catch any megs swimming out – bop them on the nose!"

"Your Majesty!" Teggs bellowed. He scattered the troops as he charged over to her, Arx and Iggy close behind. "You're being tricked! The megs are *not* sinking the island. Gastro and his dodgy plumbing are to blame!"

"How dare you?" Gastro bawled back. But his fellow terror birds looked at each other shiftily.

"It's true!" said Teggs, waving the shark-shaped swimsuit in her face. "They've been using disguises like these to make you think the megs were attacking you!"

"Er, Captain?" said Arx. He had turned, and was pointing out to sea. "It seems they really *are* attacking us!"

The waters lapping the island shore began to churn and bubble. Then twenty weird machines started emerging from the ocean. Each was like a large fish tank on wheels – and each contained a mean-looking meg. Wicked weapons gleamed on either side of the thick glass casings. Behind the first twenty came another twenty. And then *another* . . .

"They've built mobile fish tanks!" shouted Gastro. "They can go anywhere on the whole island!"

Queen Soapi bravely raised her coconut catapult. "Then let's get nutting!"

"No!" called Teggs. "You're being tricked into fighting. Stop!"

But the first coconuts had already been launched – by the terror birds standing at the front. The hairy weapons bounced harmlessly off the mobile aquariums. The bactrosaurs hooted with dismay as the super-sharks trundled onwards, aiming their guns . . .

"What can we do?" groaned Iggy.

"I don't know," said Teggs, gritting his beak. "The megs may not have started this fight – but it looks like they mean to finish it!"

Chapter Nine

THE BIG BREAKDOWN

Without warning, the megs opened fire. Big splats of dung shot out of their weapons.

"Don't be afraid!" called Queen Soapi. "Our Spotless Survival Suits will protect us!"

But they didn't.
As Teggs watched
in horror, the
dung splattered
all over the brave
bactrosaurs. It left
huge, messy stains
on their suits. Soon
there was *nothing*
spotless about them!

"Your Survival Suits don't work,
Gastro!" cried Queen Soapi. "You said
they would keep us clean!"

"So *that's* why your feathery friends
pulled me down the toilet," snarled
Iggy. "You knew that if I studied those
suits I'd learn the truth – that they're
useless!"

"Ooooh! The mess!" gasped one
bactrosaur.

"The smell!" wailed another, fainting.

"I can't stand it!" cried two more,
running into each other.

Soon the bactrosaurs were either fainting in shock or running around the beach in a giant tizzy. The megs chased after them in their terrible tank-tanks, dispensing dung with no mercy.

"Inflate your suits!" shouted the queen, pulling a special cord on her snazzy waistband. "Run into the sea and float away as fast as you can!"

The bactrosaurs did as they were told. But the suits inflated too much,

too quickly. In the
blink of an eye
the bactrosaurs
were rolling around
the beach like giant
beach balls,
completely helpless.

Only Janice the
hoof-maiden stayed
uninflated, and Queen
Soapi clung onto her for support. "You
have tricked me, Gastro!" she cried,
staring at the terror bird in disbelief.

"No!" Gastro looked like he was
about to cry. "I *know* the suits work! I
designed them myself!"

Teggs grabbed hold of him. "You
terror birds started this," he said. "Now
finish it."

"I don't know what you're talking
about!" cried Gastro. Before he could
pull free, Iggy grabbed hold of his
wings and Arx trod on his claws,

stopping him in his tracks. "Let me go! All prehistoric beasts should try to live in harmony!"

"Captain, look!" Iggy pointed to a huge tank-tank with solid-gold guns, slowly rumbling towards them. It was scattering inflated bactrosaurs in all directions. "That must be King Fin himself."

Gastro was struggling furiously. "Let go of me, Teggs!" he shouted. "We must protect Queen Soapi!"

"That's rich," Iggy snorted. "You put her in danger in the first place!"

Teggs raised his tail warningly over Gastro's head. "Terror birds, I order you to help us stop this battle. I've got your leader here!"

The terror birds sniggered. "That's what *you* think," said the one called Godfrey.

King Fin smiled wickedly as he wheeled closer and closer, his army right behind him. He aimed his dung-shooters straight at Queen Soapi. The queen bounced bravely in front of Janice to protect her. In turn, Teggs stood in front of them both.

But suddenly, the tank-tank ground to a halt. It started to shake. King Fin frowned and bubbled something *very* rude.

"Why has he stopped?" Queen Soapi wondered.

Teggs frowned. "It looks like the megs have *all* stopped!"

He was right. All over the beach, the tank-tanks had come to a halt. But it didn't look  as though the megs had *meant* to stop. Each one seemed stuck, thrashing about inside, helpless.

"The tank-tanks have broken down!" cried Queen Soapi, bouncing up and down. "We're saved!"

"Don't bet on it," sneered Godfrey.

Teggs turned to Gastro. "What have you done?"

But before Gastro could answer, a sinister shape slithered out from the sea.

It was a massive megalodon, looking so fat and stuffed that it might burst! Two terror birds went at once to help it up – and Teggs caught sight of the zipper running down its side.

"A shark costume," breathed Arx. "Just like that one we found before. Only this one still has a terror bird inside it!"

"Welcome back, Gordon." Godfrey grinned. "Did you take care of everyone in King Fin's under-sea palace?"

"Er – yeah. Everyone's locked up. We can deal with them later." Gordon waddled over in his lumpy disguise to where Gastro and the astrosaurs were standing. "Looks like the big battle is all over, eh, boss?"

Gastro only stared in angry silence.

"What's wrong, 'boss'?" sneered Teggs.

102

"Raptor got your tongue?"

"No." Gastro shook his head. "Gordon isn't talking to me."

"Correct," came a voice none of them had heard before. "He is talking to *me*!"

Iggy, Arx and Gastro jumped in the air in surprise. Queen Soapi bounced backwards in shock.

"You?" Teggs gasped. "*You* are the terror birds' boss?"

"Correct!" Janice the hoof-maiden was grinning in triumph. "My plan has worked perfectly. Nobody can stop me now!"

Chapter Ten

BOILING POINT!

"Janice!" said Queen Soapi sternly. "Stop being so naughty at once!"

"Shan't!" said Janice, sticking out her tongue. "I'm sick of acting like a faint little fairy!"

"Get that hoof-maiden!" Teggs ordered.

But Janice quickly grabbed Queen Soapi in a painful armlock. "Stay back!" she snapped. "I'm not taking any more orders from you or anyone else! You're finished, Soapi! This world now belongs to the terror birds."

"But why would you help *them*?" Arx demanded.

"I haven't. *They* have helped *me*!" She chuckled. "I could tell that Gastro's bird-brained band was getting fed up with life on the run. So I persuaded them to act like *true* terror birds. Thanks to me, the terror birds will soon inherit this planet. In return they will give me my own moon to rule over, and I shall fill it with noise and smells and machines and dirt!"

"Disgusting!" trilled Queen Soapi, helpless in her hoof-maiden's grip. "Wash your mouth out, Janice!"

"No!" She stamped her foot, making King Fin jump in his broken tank-tank. "I'm sick of acting so clean. I love muck! I love being rude! I love smelly things!"

Iggy's eyes narrowed. "So it was *you* who pulled me down the toilet."

"Correct," she sneered. "I pretended to be weak and feeble so you would never suspect me. But really I want to boss people about and make everything dirty – and that's just what I'll do!"

"So Gastro really *was* trying to help Queen Soapi," Arx realized. "He had no idea that his friends had turned against him!"

"We're fed up of eating grass and fixing toilets," said Godfrey. "Once Atlantos is ours, we shall let our rulers use it as a new nest-planet. From here they can easily raid the nearby pliosaur planets for food – YUM!"

Teggs nodded. "Then, in return, they will stop hunting you and you'll be free birds. What a nasty plan!"

"And it was all my idea," said Janice proudly. "Gastro, you are a dismal dummy. Your plumber chums have been *breaking* your precious toilet pipes, not fixing them! They have even repaired your ship in secret."

"Aha!" said Arx. "So *that's* where you got the power to block our communicators!"

"Yes," hissed Godfrey. "We weren't expecting the DSS to send you here so fast. We had to stop you getting reinforcements somehow!"

King Fin burbled and bubbled, bashing his tail helplessly against the thick plastic of his broken tank-tank.

"That's right, fish-face," sneered Janice. "We sabotaged all your tank-tanks, just like we sabotaged Gastro's Spotless Survival Suits."

"Wicked child!" gasped Queen Soapi.

Godfrey laughed. "Since no one on this island knows the first thing about technology, it was easy-peasy to trick *both* sides!"

Janice nodded. "But now it is time that this battle was brought to an end . . ."

Suddenly Teggs saw that the water in the tank-tanks was starting to bubble.

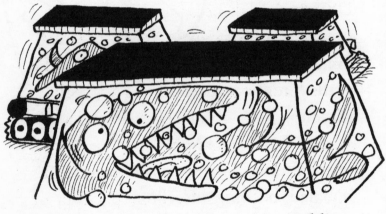

The megs trapped inside were tumbling about in alarm. "What's happening to them?" he asked. "That water looks like it's boiling."

"We told you we were sick of eating grass," rasped one of the terror birds.

"It's time we had a nice meaty dinner. Boiled shark followed by raw bactrosaurs-in-dung with astrosaurs for dessert . . ." He licked his beak. "Delicious!"

Queen Soapi finally fainted.

"You savages!" shouted Teggs. "You could at least eat us with some nice wild sea-grass!"

"Only *I* shall be spared," chuckled Janice. "And, of course, when the DSS come to investigate I shall confirm the terror birds' story: everyone on both sides was lost – and you astrosaurs got caught in the crossfire!"

"Come on, Gordon. Get out of that silly disguise," said Godfrey, pecking at the zipper on the shark suit. "Gosh, you've put on some weight, haven't you . . . ?"

"Whoaaaaaa!" Suddenly Gordon burst out of the meg outfit, like a big feathery banana squeezed from its skin.

Everyone stared in surprise. The terror bird had been thrown from his costume by a bedraggled figure in a bright orange swimsuit . . . "Gipsy!" Teggs yelled in delight. "She was hiding in that disguise with Gordon, all the time!"

"Hi, Captain!" She jabbed Godfrey in the beak and swiped another terror bird with her tail. "It was a tight fit in there, but I thought we might need to launch a surprise attack!"

"It surprised me all right!" said Iggy, beaming as he let go of Gastro and charged at the startled terror birds.

Teggs bounded after him, whirling his tail at top speed. "But, Gipsy, how did you stop Gordon from warning his friends?"

"First I beat him in battle and forced my way into his costume," she explained. "Then I told him I would yank out some *very* sensitive feathers if he didn't play along with my plan!"

Teggs struck one of the terror birds with his titanic tail. Flapping in alarm, the big bird crashed into Iggy, who socked him with his stun claws.

But by now Godfrey and Gordon had recovered. They launched into a kung-fu attack on Teggs, lashing out with their legs. Their wings whooshed through the air, ready to deliver deadly blows.

"Two against one?" sneered Teggs, blocking their ferocious kicks with his tail.

"Make that *three* against one," said a terror bird behind him, cruel talons ready to tear into Teggs's scaly skin . . .

But, suddenly, the bird was smashed senseless to the sand – by Gastro! "Make that two against two," said Gastro fiercely, standing side-by-side with Teggs. With a flurry of high-kicks and wing-chops he sent Godfrey flying. Teggs did a furious forward roll, steamrolling Gordon into the beach, leaving him in a squashed daze.

Back on his feet, Teggs saw that Iggy and Gipsy had dealt with the other two terror birds. "Good work, crew," he said. "Thanks to you too, Gastro. I'm sorry we misjudged you."

"Never mind that," said Gastro. "Where's that horrid hoof-maiden gone?"

"Look! She's getting away!" yelled Iggy.

Teggs saw that Janice was making a fast exit, climbing up a sand dune.

"Don't worry, she won't get far," called Arx. He had snapped off two dung-shooters from a tank-tank and carried one under each arm. Taking careful aim he fired both at once. With a slop, a plop and a very rude noise, Janice was engulfed in a giant ball of dung. Shrieking, she rolled helplessly back down the sand dune towards the beach.

"Got you!" cried Arx.

Iggy beamed. "Brilliant shooting!"

"Hang on, though," said Gastro. "We forgot about the tank-tanks!"

Teggs stared around. While the bactrosaurs were slowly waking from their fainting fits and floating about the beach like big balloons, the masses of megs were still trapped in their boiling, bubbling tanks. Some of them were turning red.

"The poor things," said Gipsy. "They've been tricked, they've been used – and now they're being boiled like eggs. We must get them out!"

"But there's not enough time to save them all!" said Iggy helplessly. "What can we possibly do?"

Chapter Eleven

A CLEAN GETAWAY

"The bactrosaurs," said Arx suddenly. "There are lots of them, and they're starting to wake up. *They* could help us get the megs out!"

"But will they *want* to help us?" Iggy wondered.

"Start the rescue operation, guys," said Teggs. "I'll see what I can do!"

With rocks, hooves and claws, Gipsy, Arx, Iggy and Gastro started cracking open the tank-tanks. Teggs rushed over to where Queen Soapi lay and quickly popped her inflated Survival Suit.

"Oh, my poor sweet-smelling head!"

groaned Queen Soapi. "What happened?"

"Never mind that," he said. "You and your people must help us save the megs from being boiled up like shark soup!"

"Help those slimy sea-monsters, after they splattered us with that dreadful dung?" Queen Soapi shook her head. "No!"

"They were tricked into attacking you," Teggs reminded her. "They thought you were poisoning their sea. Now they will die without your help!"

"You're wasting your time with that feeble lot, Teggs!" sneered Janice, still stuck in her giant dungball. "All they care about is keeping clean!"

"Prove her wrong," Teggs urged Queen Soapi. "Show mercy to the megs. *Please.*"

Queen Soapi gulped. Cries and wails and shrieks were starting up along the beach. Not from the helpless megs, but from the bactrosaurs – they had just realized how dirty their Survival Suits were!

"Stop moaning, you lot!" the queen cried. "We bactrosaurs are made from sterner stuff! Now, burst your silly suits – they are not tooth- or claw-proof at all. Hurry! We must help the astrosaurs rescue the megs!"

"Thanks, Your Majesty." Teggs hugged Queen Soapi, smearing her with sand as he did so. For a moment, her bottom lip wobbled.

Then she smiled and brushed the sand away. "Let's get on with it!"

The beach filled with noisy pops as the bewildered bactrosaurs bustled about the beach in deflating suits. They all mucked in to free the megs from the bubbling tank-tanks. With Gastro,

Teggs and his
crew they heaved the enormous super-
sharks back into the sea.

With all her strength, Gipsy dragged
King Fin to the water's edge. He
wriggled into the gentle waves, and
sighed with relief. "Thank you, my
dear. Can you forgive an old fool for
believing those terror
birds and locking
you up?"

Gipsy smiled.
"Everything's
OK now.
You and the
bactrosaurs
can live in
peace again."

Soon, the waters were brimming with grey fins and happy sighs. To say thank you, the megs used their sharp teeth to remove what was left of the bactrosaurs' filthy Survival Suits. The dinosaurs danced together in the water, grateful and glad to be clean again.

"There's going to be a terrible mess to clean up," said Queen Soapi.

"That's true," Teggs agreed. "Kleen Island is still sinking under the weight of all that poo and wee!"

"I think I can make a special mixture that will dissolve it," said Gastro.

"We will make it together," said Arx firmly. "And then, once the dung has disappeared, the island will rise up from the waves once again!"

"Our home will be just as it was before!" cried Queen Soapi. "Hooray!"

The bactrosaurs cheered.

"But what about all that dung in the ocean?" asked Teggs.

Gastro nodded at the pile of conked-out terror birds. "Don't worry. I will make sure these traitors clean up every polluted plop from King Fin's under-sea kingdom."

Now it was the megs' turn to cheer!

"I can help Gastro fix the plumbing for the toilets," said Iggy. "We'll make sure this can never happen again!"

"But first we must go to the terror-bird ship and switch off their jamming device," said Teggs. "I must contact the *Sauropod*. The dimorphodon will be very worried about us by now!"

"And I'm sure Admiral Rosso will be dying to know what's been going on," Gipsy agreed.

Teggs turned to Gastro. "We will have to take Janice and your ex-friends to DSS HQ to face justice. But you have proved yourself to be a very noble bird. I'm sure we can find you a happy home on any planet in the Vegetarian Sector."

"Um, that's very kind of you," said Gastro. "But if it's all right with Queen Soapi . . . I would like to stay here."

Queen Soapi grinned and gave him a hug. "Of course you can stay here, you silly great bird! This is your home, and it wouldn't be the same without you!"

Gastro hugged her back.

The planet's three suns were just starting to set. Iggy smiled through a yawn. "Well, it's been a long, long day."

"But at least we managed to *save* the day," said Teggs.

Gipsy nodded. "By getting everyone to work together."

"There's a lot more work to be done before we can all go home," Arx reminded her.

"Who wants to go home?" Iggy retorted. "I've thought of a much better use for all those catapulted coconuts — coconut smoothies. Let's have a beach party!"

"Brilliant!" said Gipsy. King Fin whooped. The megs clapped their fins together. The bactrosaurs hooted with happiness.

And Teggs smiled up at the darkening sky. The *Sauropod* was waiting up there somewhere. Waiting to take them all away on another exciting mission.

"To think I was hoping for a holiday here!" laughed Gipsy.

"I've always thought that 'holiday' was a dirty word," said Teggs. "And after all the muck we've seen around here today, I reckon I've proved it!" He cracked open a coconut and drained it dry. "The only way to *really* relax is to enjoy a crazy adventure – so let's all go off on another one soon!"

THE END

TALKING DINOSAUR!

How to say the prehistoric names
in this book . . .

STEGOSAURUS –
STEG-oh-SORE-us

HADROSAUR –
HAD-roh-sore

TRICERATOPS –
try-SERRA-tops

IGUANODON –
ig-WA-noh-don

DIMORPHODON –
die-MORF-oh-don

BACTROSAUR–
BAK-truh-SORE

MEGALODON–
may-GAL-oh-don

PLIOSAUR–
plie-oh-SORE

ASTROSAURS

BOOK NINE

THE PLANET OF PERIL

Read the first chapter here!

Chapter One

THE MONSTERS IN THE DARK

"Next stop, planet Aggadon!"
cried Captain Teggs as he
bundled aboard his
space-shuttle. A
new adventure
was beginning,
and he could
hardly wait.

Teggs and his crew had been sent to
the Tri System, a colourful collection of
worlds where millions of triceratops
had settled. New planets were being

discovered in the Tri System all the time – but sometimes, mysterious dangers were discovered with them.

That was certainly the case with the planet Aggadon.

Arx, Teggs's triceratops second-in-command, squeezed into the shuttle beside him. "I hope my niece Abbiz is all right," he said worriedly. "She went to Aggadon to help make it a nicer place for everyone coming to live there – and I haven't heard from her since!"

"She'll be fine, you'll see," said Gipsy, taking her seat behind him. "She's probably just been busy."

"Probably," agreed Iggy. He had popped his head out of a hatch in the ceiling, tangled in wires. "Either that or one of those monsters has got her!"

"Don't be daft, Iggy!" said Teggs crossly. "Of course she hasn't been got by the monsters!"

But secretly, Teggs was as worried as Arx.

At first sight, Aggadon had seemed a quiet, peaceful world. That was why so many triceratops wanted to move there. But just a few weeks after the advance group landed, a massive shower of meteorites – rocks in space – had fallen from the sky.

128

And not long after that, the first mysterious monsters had been spotted.

No one had seen them clearly – they lurked in the planet's deep forests, and their terrifying roars alone were enough to make everyone hide under their beds.

Where had the monsters come from and what did they want?

Read the rest of
THE PLANET OF PERIL
to find out just how terrifying
the monsters truly are!

Find your fantastic **ASTROSAURS** collector cards in this book. Four more cards are available in each **ASTROSAURS** book. You can also add to your collection by looking at

www.**astrosaurs**.co.uk